Big Panda, Little Panda

First edition for the United States and Canada
published 1994 by Barron's Educational Series

Text copyright © 1993 by Joan Stimson
Illustrations © 1993 by Meg Rutherford

First published in the UK by
Scholastic Publications Ltd. 1993

All inquiries should be addressed to:
Barron's Educational Series, Inc.
250 Wireless Boulevard
Hauppauge, New York 11788

Library of Congress Catalog Card No. 93-36235
International Standard Book No.
0-8120-6404-6 (hardcover)
0-8120-1691-2 (paperback)

**Library of Congress
Cataloging-in-Publication Data**

Stimson, Joan.
  Big Panda, Little Panda / Joan Stimson ; illustrated by Meg
Rutherford. – 1st ed. for the United States and Canada.
      p.   cm.
  Summary: After the arrival of his baby sister, Little Panda's mother
begins to call him Big Panda, but it takes him a while to adjust to his
new role.
  ISBN 0-8120-6404-6 (hardcover). – ISBN 0-8120-1691-2 (pbk.)
  [1. Pandas–Fiction. 2. Babies–Fiction. 3. Brothers and
sisters–Fiction. 4. Mother and child–Fiction.] I. Rutherford,
Meg, ill. II. Title.
PZ7.S86015Bi   1994
[E]–dc20   93-36235
                                                                           CIP
                                                                            AC

PRINTED IN HONG KONG
4567   987654321

Big Panda, Little Panda

Joan Stimson

Illustrated by
Meg Rutherford

BARRON'S

Ever since the little panda
could remember, he'd been
called Little Panda.

When he was tiny, his mother
fed him many times a day.
"Who's the best-looking
Little Panda in the whole
wide world?" she whispered
and held him close.

When Little Panda began to pad about, he sometimes fell and hurt himself. But Mom was always there to scoop him up. "Let's see if we can make that feel better," she said. And after a hug and a kiss, Little Panda really did feel much, much better.

And every night, when she
tucked him in, his mother
sang a lullaby. Then, when
he was not quite such a
little panda, she began to read
to him from the
old storybook.

One night Mom held Little Panda extra close.
"Who's the best-looking
Big Panda?" she whispered.

Little Panda was puzzled. He looked
around the room and shook his head.
Then his mother explained.
"Very soon there will be a new Little
Panda and I'll need a great Big
Panda to help look after us."

Finally, the new Little Panda arrived.
"Was I ever *that* little?" Big Panda asked.
"Yes, dear," Mom replied. "You were *exactly*
that little . . . and *exactly* that cute."

Mom and Big Panda took very good care of the
new Little Panda. And Big Panda even started
helping Mom with the housework.

One day Big Panda saw the wash
piled up in the laundry basket.
"I'll bet I can hang it all by
myself," he thought.
Mom smiled. "You really are
my Big Panda," she said.

Meanwhile, Little Panda was getting
bigger and bigger.
"Pretty soon she'll be ready to eat
bamboo leaves by herself," said
Big Panda.
But Mom didn't seem to be listening.
"Open wide," she said as she put
another spoonful of food into
Little Panda's mouth.

After lunch, Big Panda helped
clear off the dishes.
That's when he dropped a bowl
and hurt his paw on one
of the pieces.
"Ouch!" he cried. And he ran
to Mom and showed
her the cut.

"Oh, dear!" said Mom. "I don't think that's *too* bad, but let's get it cleaned up right away!" That's when Big Panda first noticed that Mom looked very tired.

After supper Big Panda found
the old storybook.
"Will you read to me?" he asked.
"Of course I will," said Mom.
"I love to read to my Big Panda."
But then she gave a great, big yawn.

And, before they could begin, Little Panda
started to cry.
"I won't be a minute," said Mom.

When at last she came back, Mom gave another huge yawn. She began to turn the pages of the storybook faster and faster.

"Stop!" cried Big Panda.
"You're leaving out
the best part."

But Mom was very, *very* tired.
In a few minutes, she was fast asleep.

Big Panda was tired, too.
He was tired of
housework.
He was tired of
missing story time.
And most of all, he
was tired of having a
Mom who was always tired!
"I don't like being big,"
he sniffed.

So Big Panda wrapped
Little Panda in a blanket
and tucked her in *his* bed.
Then he padded back to
Little Panda's bed and
squeezed in.

When at last she woke up, Mom looked for
a long time at the two pandas.
She remembered the unfinished story.
"I'm sorry, Big Panda," she whispered.

Next morning Mom was up early. And so
was Little Panda.
"Time to get up, Big Panda," she called.
"Where are we going?" Big Panda asked.
"Come on, we're going out," said Mom.
"We all need a change."

Mom led the way to the forest.
All day long the pandas played.
They slid down banks and climbed trees.
They chased butterflies and they munched on
tender, delicious bamboo leaves.

That night Mom was
exhausted. But she still
had a story to finish.
"Where are you, Big
Panda?" she called.

At first there was no reply.
Then suddenly a huge furry ball crashed
into view. The pandas' home shuddered.
"Good heavens!" cried Mom.
"What's that?"
The furry ball gurgled and giggled.

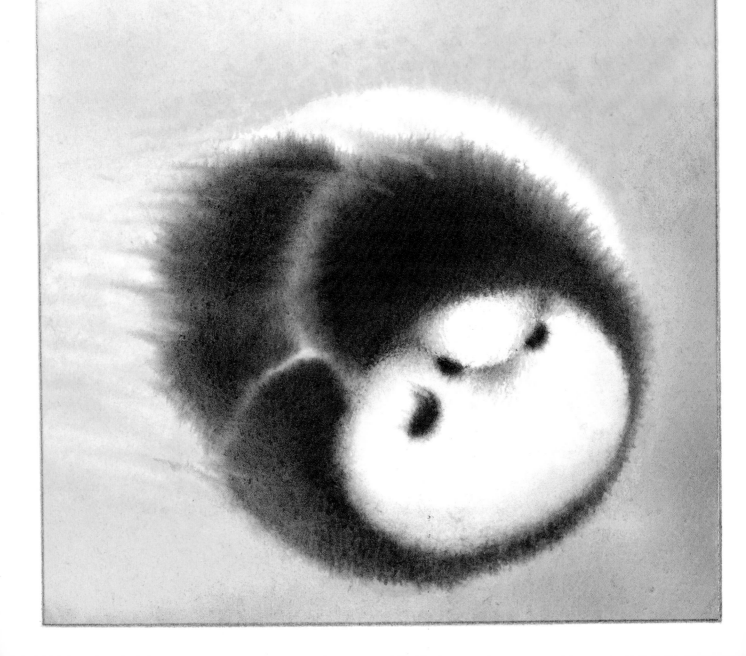

It's Little Panda and *meee*!" came the reply.
And before she knew it Mom was part of
the game.

Mom picked herself up.
She tried to get on with
the story. But Big Panda
kept interrupting.

"Look at us, look at us," he cried.
"I'm teaching Little Panda to stand
on her head."

At last the pandas quieted down and Mom
began to read.
"Oh dear," she yawned. "I can hardly keep
my eyes open."
"Never mind," cried Big Panda. He reached
across for the book. "I can read the story
tonight. Because I really am
Big Panda now . . .

And I think I'm going to like
being *big* after all."